# little Miss Twins

by Roger Hargreaves

You just couldn't tell them apart!

Who?

Why, Little Miss Twin and Little Miss Twin of course!

Who did you think?

They lived in a funny sort of a country called Twoland.

Why was it called Twoland?

You'll find out soon enough!

One morning Little Miss Twin and Little Miss Twin were having breakfast.

Two boiled eggs each!

Suddenly, there were two knocks at the door.

They both went to see who it was.

And there, standing on the doorstep, were two postmen!

"Good morning morning," they said.

People in Twoland tended to talk like that!

"Two letters for you you," they said.

"Oh good good," exclaimed the twins.

They read their letters while they finished breakfast.

After reading their letters, and after washing up, and after making their twin beds, the twins went shopping.

To Twotown!

On the way they passed two policemen.

"Hello hello," they said.

The twins bought two loaves of bread from Mrs Twiceslice, the baker's wife.

Then they went into Mr Doublechop the butcher's, and bought some sausages.

"Two pounds of your very best sausages please please," they said.

"You'll enjoy these these," smiled Mr Doublechop, as he wrapped up the sausages.

In two parcels!

Then the twins went home to Twotimes Cottage.

Oh, didn't I tell you?

That was where they lived in Twoland.

Mr Nosey was driving his car back from Happyland.

He had been to see how Mr Happy was, stayed the night, and was now on his way home.

As he was driving along he noticed a signpost he had never seen before.

It was pointing to Twoland.

"Twoland?" he thought to himself. "I've never heard of such a place!"

So, being a nosey fellow, he turned the wheel, and set off to find out where Twoland was.

He's not called Mr Nosey for nothing!

Nosey by name and nosey by nature!

It was a very warm day, and Mr Nosey began to feel decidedly thirsty.

He stopped at the first cottage he came to.

Little Miss Twin was outside, gardening.

"I say," called out Mr Nosey. "Could I possibly trouble you for a glass of water?"

"It's so hot today," he added, apologetically.

"Of course course," smiled Little Miss Twin.

"Come on in in!"

Mr Nosey couldn't quite understand why she was talking like that, but he was much too polite to mention the fact.

He got out of his car, and followed Little Miss Twin up the garden path of Twotimes Cottage.

"After you you," she said, opening the door for him.

Mr Nosey went in, and jumped.

"I thought you were behind me," he said.

"Oh no no," laughed Little Miss Twin. "She's my twin twin!"

"That's right right," giggled the other Little Miss Twin behind him.

"Am I in Twoland?" Mr Nosey asked the twins as he sipped his glass of water.

They both giggled.

"Oh yes yes," they said.

"And do you always talk like this?" he asked.

"Like what what?" they said.

"Would you like to stay for lunch lunch?" asked one of the twins.

"It's sausages sausages," added the other.

"How very kind kind," replied Mr Nosey.

Their way of talking seemed to be catching catching!

After lunch the Little Miss Twins promised to show Mr Nosey around Twoland.

They took him to the Twotown Art Gallery.

There were two of every painting!

They took him to the Twotown Hall to meet the Mayor.

Mr Doublechin!

"Welcome to our town town," he said as he shook Mr Nosey by the hand.

And then the three of them went for tea to the main hotel in Twotown.

The Ritz Ritz!

They had two cups of tea each and two sandwiches each and two cakes each.

"Let me pay," said Mr Nosey.

"Oh no no," they insisted.

"You're our guest guest," they added.

It was getting quite late when they came out of the Ritz Ritz.

"I really must be going," said Mr Nosey as he climbed into his car, which he had parked outside the hotel. "I don't like driving in the dark!"

"Lovely to meet you Mr Nosey Nosey," said one twin.

"I hope we meet again soon soon," said the other.

"Bye bye," called Mr Nosey as he drove off.

"Bye bye bye," the twins called after him.

Two days later, in Tiddletown, which was where he lived, Mr Nosey received a letter.

It had a Twoland postmark on the envelope.

And two Twoland stamps!

He opened it in great excitement.

Inside the envelope was a parking fine!

For parking his car on a double yellow line outside the Ritz Ritz in Twotown!

Which, as you know, is no place to park park!

# Fantastic offers for Little Miss fans!

**Collect all your Mr. Men or Little Miss books in these superb durable collectors' cases!**
Only £5.99 inc. postage and packing, these wipe-clean, hard-wearing cases will give all your Mr. Men or Little Miss books a beautiful new home!

**Keep track of your collection with this giant-sized double-sided Mr. Men and Little Miss Collectors' poster.**
Collect 6 tokens and we will send you a brilliant giant-sized double-sided collectors' poster! Simply tape a £1 coin to cover postage and packaging in the space provided and fill out the form overleaf.

**STICK £1 COIN HERE**
(for poster only)

**Only need a few Little Miss or Mr. Men to complete your set?** You can order any of the titles on the back of the books from our Mr. Men order line on 0870 787 1724. Orders should be delivered between 5 and 7 working days.

--- TO BE COMPLETED BY AN ADULT ---

To apply for any of these great offers, ask an adult to complete the details below and send this whole page with the appropriate payment and tokens, to: MR. MEN CLASSIC OFFER, PO BOX 715, HORSHAM RH12 5WG

☐ Please send me a giant-sized double-sided collectors' poster.
AND ☐ I enclose 6 tokens and have taped a £1 coin to the other side of this page.

☐ Please send me ☐ Mr. Men Library case(s) and/or ☐ Little Miss library case(s) at £5.99 each inc P&P

☐ I enclose a cheque/postal order payable to Egmont UK Limited for £ ...............................

OR ☐ Please debit my MasterCard / Visa / Maestro / Delta account (delete as appropriate) for £ ...........................

Card no. ☐☐☐☐ ☐☐☐☐ ☐☐☐☐ ☐☐☐☐ ☐☐☐☐  Security code ☐☐☐

Issue no. (if available) ☐  Start Date ☐☐/☐☐/☐☐  Expiry Date ☐☐/☐☐/☐☐

Fan's name: ...............................................  Date of birth: ...............................

Address: ..................................................................................................

.............................................................................................................

Postcode: ...............................

Name of parent / guardian: ...................................................................................

Email for parent / guardian: ..................................................................................

Signature of parent / guardian: ...............................................................................

Please allow 28 days for delivery. Offer is only available while stocks last. We reserve the right to change the terms of this offer at any time and we offer a 14 day money back guarantee. This does not affect your statutory rights. Offers apply to UK only.

☐ We may occasionally wish to send you information about other Egmont children's books. If you would rather we didn't, please tick this box.

**Ref: LIM 001**